# ANGLOMAN

# ANGLOMAN

## ...MAKING THE WORLD SAFE FOR APOSTROPHES!

MARK SHAINBLUM & GABRIEL MORRISSETTE
WITH A FOREWORD BY AISLIN

**NUAGE**
EDITIONS

1st printing   November 1995
2nd printing   December 1995
3rd printing   February 1996

**Additional Art Credits:**
Michel Lacombe: Inker on "Slaves of the Ice Queen" and "A Question of Danger"; background inker on "Future… Imparfait," 1990's sequences. Eric Thériault: Inker on "Future… Imparfait," 1940's sequences.

**Acknowledgements:**
Special thanks, hugs, kisses, and slaps on the back where appropriate to Max and Eva Shainblum, Brigit-Alexandre Bussière, Marc Proulx, Michel Lacombe, Eric Thériault, Mike Aragona, Jeff Boman, Matt Friedman, Lorisa Eboli, Bram Eisenthal, Marian MacNair, Terry Mosher, and, of course, J.P., for demonstrating on Oct. 30, 1995 that "Capitaine Souche" was a wildly accurate choice of name. Vive le Québec! Vive le Canada! Vive la bande dessinée! —MS

Electronic mail about Angloman may be addressed to: shainblum@vir.com Check out the Angloman Page! on the World Wide Web at: http://www.vir.com/~shainblum/angloman.htm

Printed and bound in Canada by Veilleux Impression.

Legal deposit The National Library of Canada and la Bibliothèque nationale du Québec.

**Canadian Cataloguing in Publication Data**

Shainblum, Mark, 1963-
    Angloman

ISBN 0-921833-44-X

    I. Morrissette, Gabriel, 1959-     II. Title

PS8587.H31A75 1995          C813'.54     C95-920945-X
PR9199.3.S483A75 1995

NuAge Editions
P.O. Box 8, Station E
Montréal, Québec
H2T 3A5

To Ellen Becker, who knows why.

—Mark Shainblum


A Mariette et Paul-Yves,
à Brigit pour l'année qui vient de passer et celles à venir,
et à Pierre, mon mentor.

—Gabriel Morrissette

# FOREWORD

If you don't grasp this book, you're not paying attention. Satire can't exist — never mind be understood — in a vacuum.

Angloman, son of The Anglo Survival Guide (everything comes from something), is a delightful, insightful blend of two minds (Mark Shainblum and Gabriel Morrissette) and one hand (Gabriel's) reflecting on their — our — collective experience(s) during the contemporary political/social saga that I've come to think of as… QuébéCandum.

The pols are all here: Parizeau as Le Capitaine Souche, Lucien, Jean, Preston, Pierre, Brian, etc. Several vedettes are thrown in for good measure; witness one Céline.

But we're here too — real people…

My particular favorites? The NDG Ninja and sexy Poutinette, crusader against evil, injustice and health food. Or catch the last 211 bus taking West Island Lad home.

Angloman is a successful merge of comic strip fantasy with the cutting quality of political cartooning. But, just as importantly, this book is evidence of our differences — yes — but differences that have evolved into a culture unto itself, making us all quite…inseparable.

(Terry Mosher)
November 1995
Montreal

# OFFICIALLY REGISTERED SUPERHEROES

## ANGLOMAN

***Alter Ego:*** Eaton M. McGill.
***Occupation:*** Champion of Bilingualism and Multiculturalism. Hero of the oppressed. Insurance underwriter.
***Marital Status:*** Unknown.
***Base of Operations:*** The Fortress of Two Solitudes, his secret headquarters hidden deep below the SunLife Building.
***Group Affiliation:*** La régie des superhéros et pouvoirs surhumains (often called, simply, "La régie.") Also registered with the Superhuman Abilities Directorate of Agriculture Canada.
***Height:*** 6'1"  ***Weight:*** 193 lbs.
***Powers and Abilities:*** Undetermined. Angloman is an above-average hand-to-hand combatant and he wields an array of deadly Angloweapons, including his indestructible Bilingual Shield (*Stops* everything), and his Apostrophe Darts (explosive and non-explosive). He travels by supersonic Angloplane, hangared in the Fortress of Two Solitudes and launched through a secret trap door in the roof of the SunLife Building.

## WEST ISLAND LAD

***Alter Ego:*** Jason Nirvana.
***Occupation:*** Sidekick. High school student. Post-X slacker.
***Marital Status:*** Single.
***Base of Operations:*** The Fortress of Two Solitudes, but only until about 11 pm or he'll miss the 211 bus back to Ste-Anne-de-Bellevue.
***Group Affiliation:*** La régie. The only reason Angloman even chose him as a sidekick was due to a misinterpretation of la régie's French-only rule book. Where Angloman read he *must* have a teenage sidekick at all times, the rule book actually specified that he should consider laundering his uniform at least once a week.
***Height:*** 5'6"  ***Weight:*** 117 lbs.
***Powers and Abilties:*** Annoyance. Able to listen to hard music of all types non-stop for at least fourteen hours.

# POUTINETTE

**Alter Ego:** Thérèse Papineau
**Occupation:** Co-owner, "La princesse de la pétate" restaurant, rue Ontario est. Crusader against evil, injustice, and health food.
**Marital Status:** Unknown. Possibly divorced, definitely single.
**Base of Operations:** Headquarters behind a false wall in the back of "La princesse de la pétate."
**Group Affiliation:** La régie and the Superhuman Abilties Directorate of Agriculture Canada (for now).
**Height:** 5'7"  **Weight:** 135 lbs.
**Powers and Abilities:** Above-average combatant. Armed with deadly PoutineBlaster which can immobilize an elephant in a column of poutine fifteen feet thick in seconds. Many criminals surrender merely out of fear of the cholesterol.

# The Northern Magus

**Alter Ego:** Unknown.
**Occupation:** Secret Master of the World.
**Marital Status:** Possibly.
**Group Affiliation:** Himself.
**Height:** He knows.  **Weight:** And he ain't telling.
**Powers and Abilties:** There is literally nothing the Northern Magus cannot do. He is a Secret Master of the World, and virtually everybody does his bidding at one time or another. Angloman may or may not have been set upon his mission and granted his abilties by the Northern Magus. Whether for ultimate good, or ultimate evil, we can only guess...

# POWER CHIN

**Alter Ego:** Unknown, but probably lives in Westmount.
**Occupation:** Possibly retired. Crusader against socialism, nationalism, and OTHER PEOPLE'S BLIND, SUCKING STUPIDITY!!! WHY CAN'T THEY SEE HE'S ALWAYS RIGHT??!!!
**Marital Status:** Married.
**Group Affiliation:** Not any more.
**Height:** 6'  **Weight:** 185 lbs.
**Powers and Abilities:** Power Chin's mystic Chin Guard of Power grants him superhuman powers of many kinds, but his primary ability is his laser-like focus, and his unstoppable ability to convince himself he's doing the right thing even in the face of overwhelming odds and (usually) sanity. Hates the Northern Magus, by the way. Really, *really* hates him. Has *never* been on the take. Honest.

# LE CAPITAINE SOUCHE

*Alter Ego:* Unknown.
*Occupation:* Crusader against evil, injustice, and bilingual street signs. Dedicated to *souviens* until the end of time. Alter ego career unknown. Possibly retired.
*Marital Status:* Married.
*Group Affiliation:* La régie. World Pure Wool Association.
*Height:* 5'9"  *Weight:* 295 lbs.
*Powers and Abilities:* Capitaine Souche possesses the powers of flight, super strength, and the ability to generate hot wind storms by invoking the mystic words "By Jove."

# BLOCMAN

*Alter Ego:* Unknown.
*Occupation:* Unknown. Possibly in politics.
*Marital status:* Married.
*Group Affiliation:* La régie. Anybody who'll let him be president. For now.
*Powers and Abilities:* Blocman is one of the most powerful heroes in the Angloman Universe. Affectionately known as "The Shepherd," Blocman is a formidable master of illusion who can mesmerize huge crowds and lead them like sheep. This in addition to powers of strength and flight granted by his Megablocs.

# SUPER MARIO BOY

*Alter Ego:* Unknown.
*Occupation:* Unknown. Possibly in politics.
*Marital status:* Single.
*Group Affiliation:* La régie.
*Height:* 5'8"  *Weight:* 150 lbs.
*Powers and Abilities:* Super Mario Boy is the sole survivor of the doomed planet Waffle, destroyed when illogical trade agreements with neighbouring planets collapsed. (Waffle's neighbours were often upset that the planet could never be found twice at the same coordinates.)

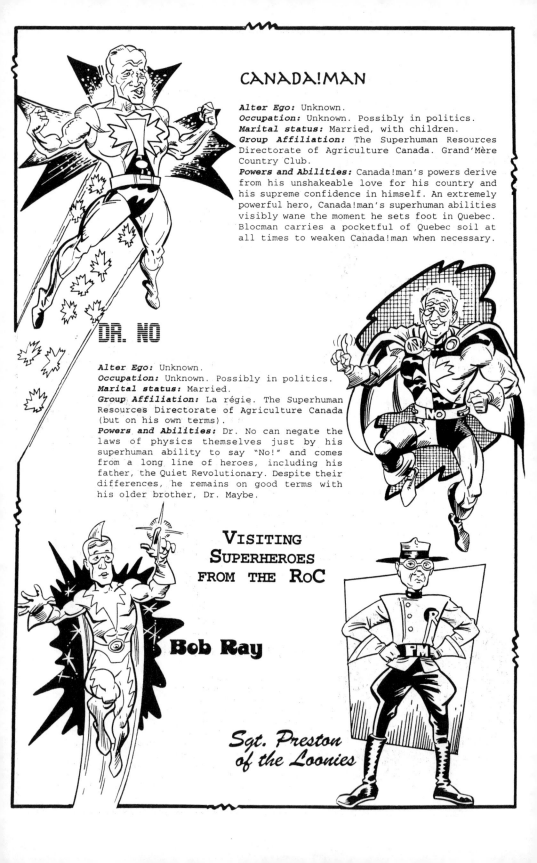

# CANADA!MAN

*Alter Ego:* Unknown.
*Occupation:* Unknown. Possibly in politics.
*Marital status:* Married, with children.
*Group Affiliation:* The Superhuman Resources Directorate of Agriculture Canada. Grand'Mère Country Club.
*Powers and Abilities:* Canada!man's powers derive from his unshakeable love for his country and his supreme confidence in himself. An extremely powerful hero, Canada!man's superhuman abilities visibly wane the moment he sets foot in Quebec. Blocman carries a pocketful of Quebec soil at all times to weaken Canada!man when necessary.

# DR. NO

*Alter Ego:* Unknown.
*Occupation:* Unknown. Possibly in politics.
*Marital status:* Married.
*Group Affiliation:* La régie. The Superhuman Resources Directorate of Agriculture Canada (but on his own terms).
*Powers and Abilities:* Dr. No can negate the laws of physics themselves just by his superhuman ability to say "No!" and comes from a long line of heroes, including his father, the Quiet Revolutionary. Despite their differences, he remains on good terms with his older brother, Dr. Maybe.

## VISITING SUPERHEROES FROM THE RoC

### Bob Ray

### Sgt. Preston of the Loonies

# PROLOGUE

A FATEFUL DAY IN JUNE. JOYFUL RESIDENTS OF QUEBEC CITY GATHER OUTDOORS IN EXPECTATION OF THEIR CITY'S SELECTION AS SITE OF THE 2002 *OLYMPIC WINTER GAMES.*

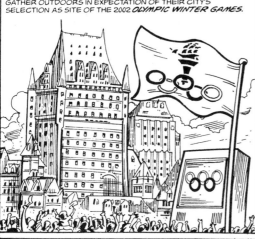

AND THE INTERNATIONAL OLYMPIC COMMITTEE'S CHOICE AS THE SITE OF THE 2002 WINTER OLYMPIC GAMES IS...

*SALT LAKE CITY!*

AWWWWWW....

AND AGAIN! AGAIN WE LOSE FACE! AGAIN OUR CITY IS HUMILIATED! FIRST WE LOSE OUR HOCKEY TEAM, OUR BELOVED NORDIQUES. NOW WE LOSE THE OLYMPICS!

AND THEM! THOSE SMUG, COSMOPOLITAN BASTARDS DOWNRIVER! THEY STILL *HAVE* THEIR HOCKEY TEAM! THEY ALREADY *HAD* THEIR DAMNED OLYMPICS!

*KRIISH*

NO MORE! NO MORE! THEY'LL *PAY!* THEY'LL LEARN WHAT HUMILIATION *REALLY* MEANS!

PROLOGUE END

# A LEGEND IS BORN

A DAY LIKE ANY OTHER IN MONTREAL.

LANGUAGE LAWS. CULTURAL TENSION. GOOD FOOD. BEAUTIFUL WOMEN. HANDSOME MEN...

...GIANT-SIZE ROBOTIC BONHOMMES CARNAVAL STOMPING THEIR WAY DOWN AVENUE MONT ROYAL.

MORT À MONTRÉAL! BANDE DE POURRIS! MONTRÉAL, ÇA PUE!

WHAT?!?!! I MEAN... IS THERE NO ONE WHO CAN SAVE US?

CRUNCH

A SCANT FEW BLOCKS AWAY, AT THE HISTORIC FORMER HEADQUARTERS OF THE *SUNLIFE ASSURANCE COMPANY.*

ONCE THE TALLEST BUILDING IN THE *COMMONWEALTH!*

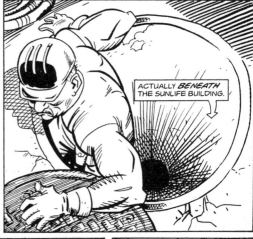

ACTUALLY *BENEATH* THE SUNLIFE BUILDING.

FAR, FAR BENEATH THE SUNLIFE BUILDING, LIES A SECRET HEADQUARTERS

A SANCTUM SANCTORUM. A HIDDEN REFUGE FROM THE *CHAOS* AND *EVIL* OF THE WORLD ABOVE...

NOTE ILCO UNICAN COMBINATION LOCK, MADE RIGHT HERE IN MONTREAL!

NO CIRCULARS PAS DE CIRCULAIRE

SO, GOOD FRIEND RONNIE, JUST YOU AND I. HOW *NASTY* I'VE BEEN, FOR CERTAIN, NO LIE.

YOGURT.

BUT I AM WHO I AM, THERE'S NO WAY TO CHANGE. AND EVEN IF POSSIBLE, WHY REARRANGE, A LIFESTYLE BOTH PLEASANT AND FUN? I ANSWER TO *ME*, TO ME AND *NO-ONE*.

AND EVEN IF RECKLESS, OR ARROGANT, A LITTLE, WHO OUT THERE IS WORTH A FLECK OF MY *SPITTLE?* WHAT POWER COULD PUNISH *ME*, SECRET MASTER OF THE EARTH? THERE'S NOTHING OUT THERE, NONE OF *MY* WORTH!

*YOU!!* I SHOULD HAVE *KNOWN!* YOU STOLE MY POOR RONNIE OUT FROM UNDER MY *NOSE!*

DEAR LADY, MY HEARING IS FINE! DO ME A FAVOUR AND TONE DOWN YOUR *WHINE!*

IT'S NOT *NICE* TO FOOL MOMMY RAYGUN!

ZZRRAP

WHOOSH

AAAAA!!!

IS IT POSSIBLE? IS IT TRUE? A CIRCUMSTANCE STRANGE AND MOST *RARE?* DID, THIS ONE TIME ALONE, THE NORTHERN MAGUS *ERR?*

POWER CHIN! WILL YOU *HALT* YOUR *RAMPAGE* OR MUST I USE ALL MEANS AT MY DISPOSAL TO *STOP* YOU?!

I'LL TAKE THAT AS A "*NO.*"

WHAM

TAKE *THAT*, AKIRA DUDE!

WHOA! WATCH OUT FOR THAT KICKBACK!

WHOOPS!

AT IT *AGAIN?* HOW MANY TIMES HAVE I TOLD YOU THAT THOSE VIDEO GAMES WILL ROT YOUR *BRAIN!*

AWW, *MAN!* HERE WE, LIKE, GO AGAIN!

Ooooo

WHAT'S *WRONG* WITH KIDS THESE DAYS?

YOU AND YOUR VIOLENT MEDIA! IT'S NOT LIKE WHEN I WAS GROWING UP WITH *GILLIGAN'S ISLAND.* NOW *THERE* WAS REAL ENTERTAINMENT!

NOW GET OUT THERE AND GO ON *PATROL!* YOU'RE ALREADY FIFTEEN MINUTES LATE.

YEAH, YEAH. AND DON'T FORGET TO SWEEP THE *ANGLOCAVE!*

*FORTRESS OF TWO SOLITUDES!*

*ANGLOCAVE!*

*FORTRESS OF TWO SOLITUDES!*

*ANGLOCAVE!*

*FORTRESS OF TWO SOLITUDES!*

*ANGLOCAVE!*

HEH, HEH. THAT ALWAYS GETS HIS GOAT, MAN.

WEST ISLAND LAD in Banzai, Dude!

THIS PAPER'S SO MUCH EASIER TO READ THESE DAYS. NO LONG SENTENCES.

HIGH ABOVE, AN OMINOUS DARK FIGURE DETACHES ITSELF FROM THE SHADOWS, READY TO POUNCE LIKE... LIKE...

...LIKE A *POUNCING THING!*

AAARRGH, DUDE!

WHAMMO

A MASSIVE BLOW TO HIS KIDNEYS *STUNS* WEST ISLAND LAD. ANYBODY ELSE WOULD PROBABLY BE *CRIPPLED* OR WORSE...

BUT HE'S A *SUPERHERO*, SO WE'RE NOT ALLOWED TO DO THAT.

AT THIS POINT, ANGLOMAN WOULD PROBABLY SAY SOMETHING LIKE "DID YOU GET THE NUMBER OF THAT *TRAIN*?"

BUT THAT'S, LIKE, SUCH A *CLICHE*, MAN.

WHAT THE? WHO'S THE DUDE DOING THE *TASMANIAN DEVIL* IMITATION?

AW, BUMMER. IT'S THAT SUPERCRIMINAL KNOWN AS THE *NOG NINJA*, PREVIOUSLY KNOWN AS THE *SNOWDON NINJA*, UNTIL HE MOVED.

AWW, MAN. I'M EVEN STARTING TO *TALK* LIKE *ANGLOMAN!*

HAYEE! KWA DWA HO KIKKOMAN *TOYOTA!*\*

"I HAVE COME TO CHALLENGE YOU TO A TEST OF SKILL!"

[PLEASE READ VERY QUICKLY WITHOUT INFLECTION, AND WITHOUT BREATHING BETWEEN WORDS.]

OH GREAT. AND ME WITHOUT MY *ANGLOMACE* AND MY *ANGLO BRASS KNUCKLES!*

GUESS I'LL JUST, LIKE, HAVE TO DO THIS THE OLD FASHIONED WAY.

AT LEAST I'LL PROVE TO ANGLOMAN THAT I'M NOT A TOTAL WUSS SLACKER!

GOTTA REMEMBER MY *SUPERHERO DIALOGUE 101!*

PREPARE TO MEET YOUR, LIKE, *DOOM* FOUL VILLAIN.

DAMN, THAT'S *CORNY!*

KWA WASSABE!

*SWISH SWISH*

*SWISH SWISH SW SHW*

"SHUT UP AND *FIGHT!*

GET OUT OF MY FACE! THIS ISN'T *METHOD* ACTING SCHOOL!

TOUCHY. TOUCHY. TOUCHY.

IMAGINE THE, LIKE, NERVE OF THOSE *HOLLYWOOD* TYPES. LET A CANADIAN BOY GET OUT OF THE *COUNTRY* AND, LIKE, SEE WHAT HAPPENS TO HIM.

AND IT'S NOT LIKE HE'S EVEN A *REAL* ACTOR LIKE *WILLIAM SHATNER.*

OMYGOD! IT'S AN *EMERGENCY!*

BEEP BEEP

GOTTA MOVE! GOTTA MOVE!

WHEW! ALMOST MISSED THE LAST *211* TO THE WEST ISLAND! MAN I CAN'T WAIT TILL I GET A *DRIVERS LICENSE.*

211 - STE-ANNE

JUST WISH I COULD *RIDE* THE BUS LIKE A NORMAL PERSON! BUT THIS COSTUME IS JUST TOO *DORKY*, MAN! WHAT IF I SAW SOMEBODY I *KNEW?*

ANYWAY! SURFING THE T-CAN ALL THE WAY HOME! *COOL!*

ANGLOMAN SAYS:

DON'T TRY THIS AT HOME, KIDS!

AND TAKE YOUR *VITAMINS!*

END

RUE ONTARIO, IN DEEPEST DARKEST MONTREAL EAST, WHERE NO UNILINGUAL ANGLOPHONE WOULD *DARE* SHOW HIS FACE FOR FEAR OF BEING LABELLED A "HOST OF A TABERNACLE OF A BLOKE..."

LA PRINCESSE DE LA
HAMBURGERS
HOT DOGS
PIZZA
POUTINE
SMOKED MEAT
PETATE
BzT BzT BzT
DÉJEUNER
BUVEZ PARSI!

*LUNCHTIME* AT A FAMOUS LOCAL EATERY WHERE CUSTOMERS SATIATE THEMSELVES ON CHOLESTEROL IN ITS MANY FORMS!

LE CHOLESTÉROL EST NOTRE AMI
IL NE FAUT PAS EN AVOIR POUR
M. BEURRE DIT BOUFFE-MOI!
POP-POP
SIZZLE
SIZZLE
SIZZLE

MOST FAVOURED OF THESE DELICACIES IS *POUTINE*, A WONDROUS MÉLANGE OF FRIES, GRAVY AND CHEESE CURD... MORE THAN THE SUM OF ITS PARTS! A HOLY EXPERIENCE IN JUNK FOOD DEGUSTATION!

HERE YOU GO, TI-CUL! *POUTINE* WITH EXTRA GRAVY AND CHEESE! *BEST* IN THE CITY!

WHAT A DAY, MA PETITE THÉRÈSE! MY FEET ARE JUST *KILLING* ME!.

ME TOO, TANTE HORTENSE! I'M *EXHAUSTED*!

TOO EXHAUSTED TO GO ON PATROL AS *POUTINETTE* TONIGHT!

# POUTINETTE in SLAVES OF THE ICE QUEEN

ELSEWHERE, AT THE SUMPTUOUS, YET UNDERSTATED ESTATE OF *CLAUDINE DIONNE* AND *RENÉ DIABOLIN.*

FONY

OH IT WAS THE *HAPPIEST* DAY OF MY *LIFE!*

SOB! SOB! SOB! OH, IT WAS *SO* BEAUTIFUL!

AND EVERYTHING WAS SO *DIGNIFIED!*

CLAUDINE, SWEETUMS, ARE YOU IN HERE?

CLIK

OKAY BOYS, THAT'S *ALL* FOR NOW. SAME TIME *TOMORROW!*

SNAP

AND NOW IT'S *MY TURN!* NOW YOU *SUFFER!*

A SONG AS OLD AS TIME...!

NOOOO! NOT *THAT!!* ANYTHING BUT THAT!!

BLOOD SUGAR RISING!!

I CAN'T *BEAT* HER! SHE'S GOING TO *KILL* ME WITH SACCHARINE *MUSIC!*

WAIT, I'VE *GOT* IT!

BOO! HISS! HISS!

YOU *DARE* TO BOO QUEBEC'S PRINCESS OF POP?! DYING TO *MY* MUSIC IS AN *HONOUR* FEW SUPERHEROES COULD *EVER* HOPE TO ACHIEVE!

BUT THAT'S JUST IT, MA CHÈRE, YOU'RE NOT *QUEBEC'S* PRINCESS OF POP ANYMORE! YOU SING IN *ENGLISH* ALMOST ALL THE TIME NOW!

YOU'VE BECOME AN *ANGLOPHONE!!*

NOOOOOO!!!!

WELL, THERE GOES MY *MEAL TICKET.*

HMMM. I WONDER IF *POUTINETTE* CAN SING?

END

# CAPITAINE SOUCHE

## in A QUESTION OF DANGER

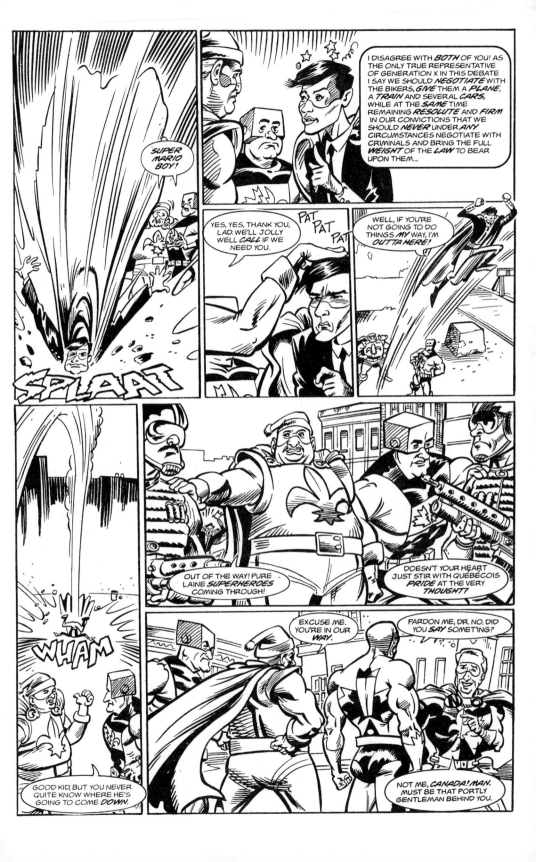

END

FUTURE...imparfait

WHAT HAVE YOU *DONE?* WHERE ARE WE?

DON'T YOU SEE? IS IT BEYOND YOUR *KEN?* THE QUESTION'S NOT *WHERE,* THE QUESTION IS *WHEN!*

I DON'T FOLLOW YOU.

ARE YOU FOR *REAL?* WHAT MAKES YOU *TICK?* THE YEAR'S *'48* DON'T YOU SEE, OR ARE YOU TOO *THICK?*

1948!!!

HEY!!

JOY! RAPTURE! I HAVE BEEN RETURNED TO MY *RIGHTFUL PLACE!* TO HEAVEN ON EARTH! TO A NIRVANA WHERE EVERYBODY SPEAKS *ENGLISH* IF THEY KNOW WHAT'S *GOOD* FOR THEM!

WAIT ANGLOMAN, HE'S NOT YOUR *JOB.* NEITHER ARE THUGS WHO MURDER AND *ROB!*

TIME WENT AWRY, THINGS WENT ASTRAY. YOU'RE HERE TO FIX TIME UP, OR HERE YOU SHALL *STAY!*

Y'KNOW, I'M GETTING PRETTY @#%ING TIRED OF YOUR LAME *RHYMES,* DUDE.

QUIET, LAD. DON'T *UPSET* HIM.

MAGUS, WE DON'T *BELONG* HERE. THIS *ISN'T* OUR TIME AND PLACE. TAKE US HOME.

NO, ANGLOMAN. NO, I THINK NOT. SAVE US FROM *TIM,* SAVE US FROM *ROT.*

YOU'LL UNDERSTAND, YOU WILL, IN DUE *TIME.* AND *BOY,* WATCH YOUR SHARP TONGUE ABOUT ME AND MY *RHYME.*

POP!

*"BOY?!"* WHO DOES THAT DUDE THINK HE IS?

HE'S A SECRET MASTER OF THE WORLD, LAD. IT'S BETTER NOT TO UPSET SOMEONE WHO CAN TURN YOU INTO A *MOSQUITO* AND THEN *SQUASH* YOU.

"SAVE US FROM TIM? SAVE US FROM ROT?" WHAT'S *THAT* SUPPOSED TO MEAN?

OH WELL, AT LEAST, LIKE, HE LEFT US THE *ANGLOPLANE.*

SO, LIKE, WHAT'RE WE SUPPOSED TO *DO,* A-MAN?

*DARNED IF* I KNOW, LAD.

YEAH, IF ANYBODY'LL BE "DARNED," IT'LL BE *YOU,* DUDE.

Y'KNOW, A-MAN, EVERY EPISODE OF STAR TREK I'VE EVER SEEN SAYS IT'S, LIKE, *DANGEROUS* TO MESS WITH THE *PAST!* YOU CAN, LIKE, KILL YOUR OWN *GRANDFATHER* OR SOMETHING.

HAHAHA! STAR TREK! YOU CRAZY KIDS! THAT'S *TV,* LAD! THIS IS *REAL LIFE!*

RIGHT. SAYS THE DUDE WITH THE BIG "A" ON HIS CHEST.

WHAT'S YOUR *POINT?*

SIGHHHH. NEVER MIND, DUDE. NEVER MIND.

SOON, IN A SECLUDED SPOT ON *MOUNT-ROYAL.*

THE PLANE'LL BE SAFE HERE. WE'VE GOT TO GET SOME *STREET CLOTHES!* AND I KNOW *JUST* THE PLACE TO GO!

CAN YOU FEEL IT, LAD? THE *HUSTLE?* THE *BUSTLE?* THE POST-WAR *OPTIMISM?* THE SENSE OF *PRIDE* AND *HOPE* FOR THE FUTURE?

THEY'LL LEARN, DUDE. THEY'LL *LEARN.*

**Panel 1**

SOMETIME LATER, ON THE ROOF OF THE *EATON'S* BUILDING.

BUT, LIKE, THEY'RE NOT GOING TO *WANNA* DO THIS, BIG A!

SOMETIMES WE DON'T LIKE WHAT'S *GOOD* FOR US, LAD. WE'LL HAVE TO TAKE SOME *EXTREME* MEASURES.

**Panel 2**

AND ALL THROUGH THE NIGHT, MYSTERIOUS SOUNDS REVERBERATED FROM THE EATON'S BUILDING.

WHtttr  ZAP  KRAK  ZWEEE  BIPBIPBI  BOUM  BANG  SIZZLE  BIP BIP BIP  BANG  ZWEEE  POP  SNAP  BANG  BANG

**Panel 3**

BRIGHT AND EARLY THE NEXT MORNING, AS EATON'S WORKERS CHEERFULLY STREAM IN TO BEGIN ANOTHER DAY...

GOOD MORNING, CLASS. I'M MR. *ANGLOMAN*. THIS IS MR. WEST ISLAND LAD. OUR LESSON TODAY IS *POLITENESS IN FRENCH*. NOW, I'M PREPARED TO KEEP YOU *AFTER SCHOOL* IF YOU DON'T BUCKLE DOWN AND STUDY! SO *HOP TO IT!*"

TODAY: FRANÇAIS 101

Today's lesson:
-puis-je vous aider?
-est-ce que je peux vous aider?
-qu'ossé qu'on peut faire pou' toué?

STOP

BIP!

SLAM

BUT...  BUT...  BUT...

**Panel (lower row)**

A IS FOR ARGENT  B IS FOR BÉCOSSE  C IS FOR CHAR  $$$

BUT... BUT... BUT... BUT...

VERY GOOD! THIS IS A "BOTTE!"

DON'T YOU FIND IT A LITTLE, LIKE, *WEIRD* THAT WE JUST *HAPPENED* TO HAVE EVERYTHING WE NEEDED TO TEACH COLLEGE-LEVEL *FRENCH* IN THE ANGLOPLANE?

A *SUPERHERO* IS ALWAYS *PREPARED!*

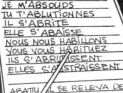

JE M'ABSOUDS
TU T'ABLUTIONNES
IL S'ABRITE
ELLE S'ABAISSE
NOUS NOUS HABILLONS
VOUS VOUS HABITUEZ
ILS S'ABRUTISSENT
ELLES S'ABSTRAISSENT

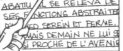

ABATTU IL SE RELEVA DE SES FONCTIONS ABSTRAITE... SEREIN ET FERME... MAIS DEMAIN NE LUI S... SI PROCHE DE L'AVENI...

ALOUETTE, GENTILLE ALOUETTE, ALOUETTE, JE TE PLUME

ALL RIGHT, BY JOVE!? WHAT'S *GOING ON* HERE!?

MAJOR *WESTMOUNT!* THANK *GOODNESS* YOU'RE HERE! THEY'RE TEACHING US *FRENCH!*

THE *FIENDS!*

MAJOR WESTMOUNT?! MY GOD! IT'S *DAD!*

SMASHING

WELL? *EXPLAIN* YOURSELF, SIR! WHY ARE YOU DISRUPTING THE *NATURAL ORDER* OF THINGS?

UHH ... UHHH...

WHAT DID I TELL YOU? THE FUTURE ISN'T DYSTOPIAN *ENOUGH* FOR THEM!

THEY WANT TO MAKE IT *WORSE* BY STARTING BILINGUALISM *EARLY!*

BILINGUALISM, BRRR!

YOU WERE RIGHT, GOOD FELLOW. THESE MISCREANTS FROM THE TERRIBLE *FUTURE* CANNOT EVEN *SPEAK* PROPERLY!

ALL RIGHT YOUNG FELLOWS. DO YOU END YOUR *DEVIANT* BEHAVIOUR *NOW,* OR MUST I *THRASH* YOU?

OR MUST WE *BOTH* THRASH YOU?

ALLÉLUI

ALLÉLUIA

LE *CAPITAINE CATHOLIQUE!* WHAT ARE *YOU* DOING WEST OF ST. LAWRENCE STREET?

I HEARD RUMOURS THAT THE EATON'S STAFF WERE BEING TAUGHT *FRENCH!* THIS *CANNOT* BE TOLERATED! IF *ANYBODY* CAN SPEAK FRENCH, THEN *EVERYBODY* WILL SPEAK FRENCH!

AND THEN HOW WILL WE KNOW WHO IS *REALLY* FRENCH AND WHO *ISN'T?*

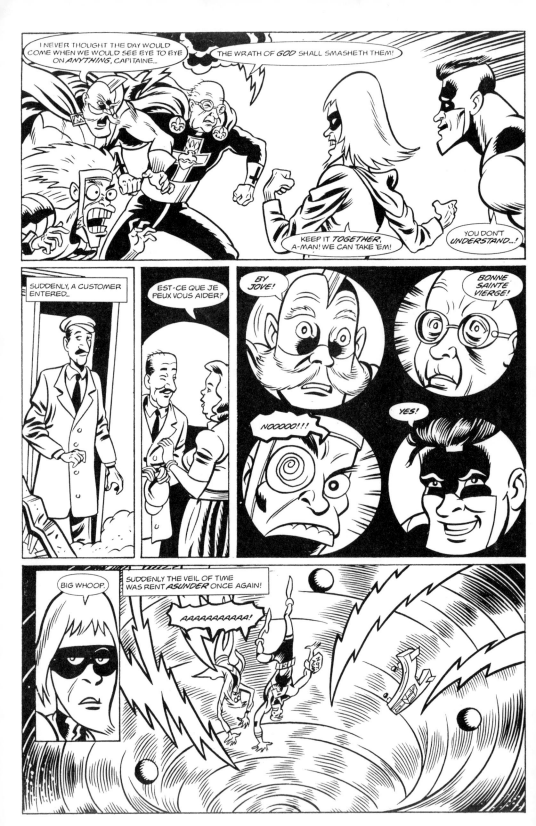